For Gemk,

Whose endless supply of ideas and honest critique made this possible.

感謝 Gemk

源源不絕的靈感及誠懇的建議讓這一切成真。

The Magic Mirror

會魔法

的鏡子

Coleen Reddy 著

沈苑苑 繪

薛慧儀 譯

三民書局

One day as Mary was walking home from school,
she went to the market.
Her mother had told her to buy some mangoes.
But she saw something special.

有天，瑪莉從學校回家的路上，順道去了市場。
媽媽要她買一些芒果。
但是她在市場裡看見了一樣很特別的東西。

3

She saw a beautiful mirror.

It was only $20. She bought it.

She forgot all about the mangoes.

She went home and put the mirror on her wall.

她看見一面很漂亮的鏡子，
而且只要二十塊錢而已耶！
於是她買下鏡子，
把芒果忘得一乾二淨。
回到家裡，她把鏡子掛在牆上。

When she looked in the mirror, she saw something weird.
She could see her face but she could also see another face.
It was the face of an old woman.

FAMOUS MODEL

她照照鏡子，發現有點不對勁。
她不但看見自己的臉，還看見另外一張臉！
那是一個老女人的臉！

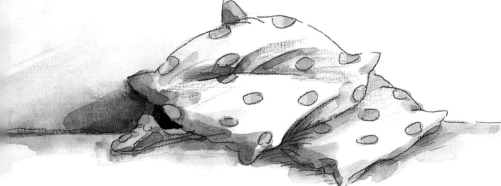

Mary was scared.

"Don't be afraid," said the face.

"I am the Magic Mirror. I will grant you three wishes."

Mary wasn't scared anymore. She smiled.

瑪莉嚇壞了。
「別怕別怕，」那張臉說，
「我是魔鏡，我可以幫妳實現三個願望喔！」
瑪莉不再害怕了，她露出了微笑。

9

"Cool," said Mary. "Okay, I want lots of money and candy...."
"Stop," said the Magic Mirror. "Not those kind of wishes. I can only grant wannabe wishes. You can wish for what you want to be."

「酷！」瑪莉說。「好，那我要很多的錢和糖果……」
「等等！」魔鏡說，「不是那種願望啦！我只能讓妳實現
想當什麼人的願望，妳可以許願變成自己想要當的人。」

"I see," said Mary. "I want to be a... a... a MODEL.
I want to be a beautiful, famous model."
"Okay, it shall be so," said the Magic Mirror.
"Now close your eyes."
Mary closed her eyes.

「我懂了，」瑪莉說。「那我要當一個…一個模特兒，
我要當一個又漂亮又出名的模特兒。」
「沒問題，妳的願望立刻就會實現。」魔鏡說。
「現在閉上妳的眼睛吧！」
於是瑪莉把眼睛閉上。

When she opened her eyes, she was a tall, thin, beautiful model.
She was wearing cool clothes and people were taking photographs of her.
They took hundreds of photographs.

當她睜開眼睛的時候，已經是個又高又瘦的漂亮模特兒了呢！
她穿著很時髦的衣服，而且人們不停地對她拍照。
他們照了起碼有好幾百張呢！

Finally, Mary took a break.
She was tired and hungry.
She saw some hamburgers on the table.
She picked one up to eat.

16

好不容易可以休息了，瑪莉覺得又累又餓。
她看見桌上有一些漢堡，
於是便拿起一個，準備要大快朵頤。

"Stop," said a woman. "You cannot eat that. You'll get fat.
You can eat this," she said.
She gave Mary a small piece of lettuce.
"That's not enough. I want more," said Mary.
"Okay, you can have two pieces of lettuce," said the woman.

「等等！妳不能吃那個，會變胖的！妳只能吃這個。」
一個女人說。她給瑪莉一片小小的萵苣。
「這怎麼夠嘛！我還要再多一點。」瑪莉說。
「好吧，那妳可以吃兩片萵苣。」那女人說。

Mary groaned and her stomach grumbled.

"Can I have some Coca Cola to drink?" asked Mary.

"No, you can only drink water," said the woman.

瑪莉抱怨了起來，而且她的肚子也在咕嚕咕嚕地叫著。

「我能不能喝點可樂呀？」瑪莉問。

「不行，妳只能喝水。」那個女人說。

20

Mary said, "Magic Mirror, this isn't working.
I want to be a... a... a MOVIE STAR."
She closed her eyes again and when she opened them
she was on a movie set.
Someone was yelling at her. It was the director.

瑪莉說：「魔鏡呀！這樣我受不了！我要當一個…一個電影明星。」
她再次閉上眼睛，等她張開的時候，已經站在拍電影的現場了。
有個人正對她大吼大叫，原來那個人是導演。

"Why are you late? You're always late! Let's go.

One, two, three and ACTION!" screamed the director.

Mary said her lines. It was a sad part of the movie and she had to cry.

She tried her best to cry but she couldn't.

She couldn't pretend.

「妳為什麼遲到？妳每次都遲到！快點快點！要拍了！
一、二、三、開始！」導演大喊。
瑪莉開始念台詞，這是電影裡一段悲傷的場景，她要哭出來才行。
但不論怎麼嘗試，她就是哭不出來，她沒辦法假裝自己很傷心。

"I want to see some real tears," yelled the director.

"If you don't cry right now, you will never work in Hollywood again."

Mary got so scared that she really did start crying.

"Good, good," said the director.

26

「我要看到真的眼淚！」導演大吼。「如果妳現在
哭不出來，妳就永遠都別想再待在好萊塢啦！」
　　瑪莉嚇壞了，結果她真的哭出來了。
　　「嗯，很好，很好。」導演說。

27

"Magic Mirror," screamed Mary. "I hate being an actress.
I want to be a... a...."
"Wait," said the Magic Mirror. "You only have one wish left.
Use it wisely."
"I want to be... ME," said Mary.

「魔鏡呀！」瑪莉大喊，「我討厭當演員啦！我要當…當一個……」

「等等喔！」魔鏡說。「妳只剩下一個願望了，要好好想清楚喔！」

「我要當…我自己！」瑪莉說。

She opened her eyes and she was back in her bedroom.

The magic face in the mirror had disappeared.

But Mary didn't mind that it wasn't a magic mirror anymore.

She could eat what she wanted, do what she wanted to

and she only needed to cry when she was really sad.

She looked in the mirror and was happy to see her own true reflection.

她張開眼睛，發現自己回到了房間，魔鏡裡的那張臉也消失了。
雖然它不再是魔鏡了，但是瑪莉一點也不在意。
她可以吃自己想吃的東西，做自己想做的事，
而且只需要在真正傷心的時候才掉眼淚。
她照照鏡子，很高興看到自己本來的模樣。

31

我的大夢想

在左邊的鏡子貼上自己現在的照片，在右邊的鏡子畫上自己將來想成為的人！

個人小檔案

名字：　　　　　　性別：　　　　　　生日：

星座：　　　　　　身高：　　　　　　體重：

專長：　　　　　最擅長的科目：　　　　最愛吃的東西：

偶像：　　　　　最喜歡的電視節目：　　　最喜歡的書：

　　　我是　　　　　　　，今年已經　　歲了。我覺得自己
在　　　　　方面很厲害，爸爸媽媽、老師和同學都很
稱讚我，讓我覺得自己真得很棒，將來一定可以成為
　　　　　　　　　　　。首先，為了達到目標，我要
　　　　　　　　　　　　　　　　　　　，然
後還要　　　　　　　　　　　　　　　　　，
最後再　　　　　　　　　　　　　　　就
可以成為我心目中的　　　　　了！我對自己有信心！
我一定要努力地達成目標，樂觀地向前走！

加油！加油！加加油！

我的簽名：

見證人：

（加蓋手印）

（請爸爸或媽媽簽名）

生字表

全新創作 英文讀本
帶給你優格（yogurt）般，青春的酸甜滋味！

Teens' Chronicles

愛閱雙語叢書

青春記事簿

大維的驚奇派對／秀寶貝，說故事／杰生的大秘密
傑克的戀愛初體驗／誰是他爸爸？
叛逆大維打工記／外星老師來上課／耶！放假了！

你我身上純真的影子，
透過一篇篇幽默風趣的故事重現，
推薦你這套青春無悔的創作系列，
讓愛玫、杰生、大維、凱爾、海倫、傑克，
帶你進入他們的世界，品味另一種學習英語的全新感受。

國家圖書館出版品預行編目資料

The Magic Mirror:會魔法的鏡子 / Coleen Reddy
著; 沈苑苑繪; 薛慧儀譯.－－初版一刷.－－臺
北市; 三民，2003
　　面; 公分－－(愛閱雙語叢書.二十六個妙朋
友系列) 中英對照
　ISBN 957-14-3766-2 (精裝)

　1.英國語言－讀本

523.38 92008806

© **The Magic Mirror**
—— 會魔法的鏡子

著作人　Coleen Reddy
繪　圖　沈苑苑
譯　者　薛慧儀
發行人　劉振強
著作財
產權人　三民書局股份有限公司
　　　　臺北市復興北路386號
發行所　三民書局股份有限公司
　　　　地址／臺北市復興北路386號
　　　　電話／(02)25006600
　　　　郵撥／0009998-5
印刷所　三民書局股份有限公司
門市部　復北店／臺北市復興北路386號
　　　　重南店／臺北市重慶南路一段61號
初版一刷　2003年7月
　編　號　S 85646-1
　定　價　新臺幣壹佰捌拾元整
　　　行政院新聞局登記證局版臺業字第○二○○號

ISBN　957-14-3766 2　（精裝）